Birthday Chickens

by Shirley Kurtz
illustrated by Cheryl Benner

Good Books

Intercourse, PA 17534
Printed in Mexico

C.I.P. data may be found on page 32

For birthdays there was always a cake, and whatever the birthday child wanted for supper.

This time the boy decided on eggs. "Eggs, my goodness!" his mother said, but she fixed everybody some eggs.

The present hadn't come yet, the boy's father said. Maybe tomorrow. They'd have to go pick it up at the post office.

Pick it up? Something too big to fit in the mailbox?

It was two whole days until the post office called.

The package wasn't real big, and there were holes.

Chicks!

At home the boy ran to the shed for a bigger box, and the father strung up a light. "To keep them warm," he said. "Because they don't have their mother."

The chicks liked their mash all right, but what they really gobbled up were the bugs. It was like a football game whenever the boy brought a bug. One chick would pounce on it and then race around the box with the others chasing and attacking and grabbing with their beaks.

"I can't believe how fast they grow," the sister said. "All that sweet fuzz gone." The father was putting up a fence and making a coop out of old boards from the pile behind the shed.

It was a wonderful coop. They all said so, even the mother. In the late evening while the father hammered the last boards, the boy held the light for him and hooted at the owls hooting at each other.

Couldn't the owls get his chickens? he wondered later on, in bed.

"We'll hope they don't," his father said.

Now the boy could be in with his chickens.

He had to keep finding things for them to eat. Kitchen garbage and moldy leftovers. Whatever got caught in the mousetraps down in the cellar. Worms from the garden when the father was digging up the potatoes. "Worms, ugh," the sister said.

When the chickens saw the boy coming with more garbage, they'd gabble and shove and jam so close to the fence there wasn't any place to dump the stuff except right on top of them.

The fence was supposed to be keeping the chickens in, not just their enemies out. But they were getting strong wings and long scratchy claws.

"We'll have to clip their feathers," the father said. "Just one wing, like this. It doesn't hurt. It's like getting a haircut."

"Those are my good scissors!" the mother said.

Whenever a chicken dug under the fence, the boy had to go catch it and find the hole and plug it up, even if he was right in the middle of his supper.

Did chickens sleep with their heads under their wings? the boy wondered. Like the birds in poems? One night, quite late, he and the mother sneaked through the moonlight, just to see.

But they couldn't tell. The chickens all woke up.

Now the last things in the garden had been picked. The boy could let the chickens out in the evenings to scrabble and peck in the weeds. "Make sure that gate's propped open," his father would warn. When it got dark the chickens would go scurrying back to the coop.

The father would shut them up later in the night, before he came up to bed, so nothing could get at them.

But once the boy forgot to prop the gate.

He forgot until he was in bed himself. Maybe he'd even slept some. He could hear his father calling for him to come down here right this minute.

The chickens were in a huddle under the coop. The boy had to crawl under and grab them.

Another night nobody forgot. The boy was safe under the covers.

He was sure he was dreaming, but then he sat straight up in his bed. All that noise coming in his window! Such a squawking and carrying on! His father was already running downstairs and grabbing the flashlight.

The chickens were down off their roost, still flapping and clucking but not any of them hurt, except for the one. It was dead.

The boy cried.

In the morning he could see the tracks. A mink, the father guessed. Or maybe a weasel. "I'm real sorry," he said. "We'll have to tighten up the coop."

"I don't see how those chickens can eat that corn you've been giving them," the boy's mother said one day. "It's too hard. Chickens don't have any teeth."

"But they have gizzards," the boy said. He knew more than she did. He'd read about gizzards in the encyclopedia.

"Well, I still think that corn is too hard," the mother said. "We've not gotten a thing out of those chickens yet. Maybe you're not feeding them right."

She cooked some of the corn until it was fat and mushy, and the boy carried it out to the chickens for their Thanksgiving feast. They couldn't even cackle, they were gobbling it up so fast.

Near Christmas the boy's father built some boxes out of wood from the junkpile and put them in the back of the coop. "For nests," he told the boy. "It's getting to be time."

And then after Christmas they were taking the tree down, and the sister said they should save the popcorn strings for the chickens. When the boy took the popcorn out to the coop, he found the very first egg.

It was pretty much like a regular egg.

The next day there were two eggs and the next day four. Then more and more.

"But you can't be hauling them in your pockets," the boy's mother said. "My goodness."

The eggs were always warm in his hands. The chickens all wanted to sit on the same nest, so they had to take turns. There could be four or five eggs under one chicken and not any of them hers, until she laid one herself.

Once the boy saw a chicken's egg come out. The chicken cackled right in his face.

When there got to be too many eggs for the boy to remember them all, he made a chart. Each day he wrote down the number he'd collected.

"You'd think those chickens would slow down some on these real cold days," his father said. "But it looks like they're keeping pretty busy."

The boy put up a big sign. FOR SALE: BROWN EGGS FRESH FROM THE CHICKENS. The money had to go into a jar for more feed. Because he wouldn't be getting his breakfast if the chickens didn't get theirs. They were as greedy as ever.

The funny thing was, they were always just as happy with the bugs and worms and garbage as he was with his eggs. As many as he wanted and cooked whichever way he liked and not just on his birthday.

Directions for Making a Birthday Cake
Like the Boy's, and Other Recipes

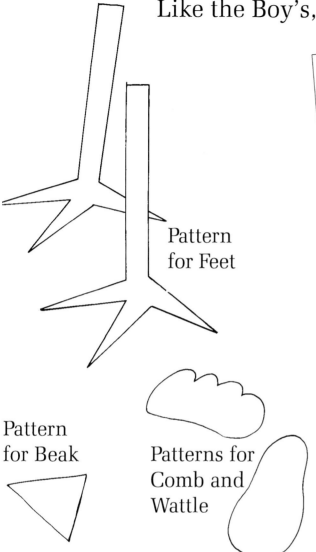

Pattern for Feet

Pattern for Beak

Patterns for Comb and Wattle

Birthday Cake

Beat till smooth:
¾ cup margarine
1½ cups sugar
3 eggs

Add & beat:
2 tsp. vanilla
3 cups flour

Add & beat:
2 tsp. baking powder
1 tsp. baking soda
½ tsp. salt
1½ cups sour milk

Add & beat:

Pour batter into two 8- or 9-inch greased layer pans. Bake at 350°, remove from pans, and cool.

Cake, continued

Cut one layer in half. Cut pieces out of the other layer. (You can eat the leftovers.) Lay chicken parts together on large tray and frost.

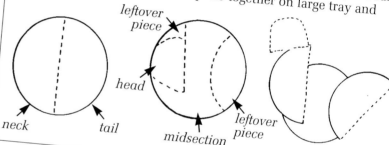

leftover piece

head

neck *tail* *midsection* *leftover piece*

Frosting, continued

Frost chicken all over with the chocolate frosting, then pile and streak the chicken's mid-section and tail end with white frosting, for a feathery effect. Add a gumball eye; beak and feet cut out of yellow construction paper; comb and wattle cut out of red construction paper; and some real chicken feathers, if you can find them.

Frosting and Trimmings for Cake

Beat till creamy:
½ cup margarine
4 cups confectioner's sugar
1 tsp. vanilla
4 Tbsp. milk (approximately)

Put about one-third of the frosting into another bowl. To the frosting left in the mixing bowl add 5 Tbsp. cocoa and a little more milk and beat till creamy.

Omelet

Beat 2 or 3 eggs and pour into large, hot, buttered skillet. Cook eggs on underside. Flip all in one piece and cook on other side. Remove from heat. Quickly top eggs with chopped onions, tomatoes, peppers, grated cheese, bits of ham or bacon (whatever you think sounds good), keeping everything to one side. Fold other half over, atop the chopped things, and let sit till cheese has melted.

Stuffed Eggs

Cut hard-cooked eggs in half lengthwise and collect all the yolks in a bowl. Smash yolks with a fork. Mix with mayonnaise and a little mustard. Put the yolks back into their holes and sprinkle with paprika.

Red Beet Eggs

Eat some of the beets out of a jar of pickled beets. Put several hard-cooked eggs in the jar with the remaining juice and beets, and store in the refrigerator for a day or two. The eggs will pickle and turn red.

Campfire Eggs

In the bottom of a small brown paper bag put several half-strips of bacon. Fold bag shut. Poke the end of a hot dog stick through the upper part of the bag and hold it over red-hot coals till bacon is partly cooked and bottom of bag is coated with grease. Remove from fire and break one or two eggs atop the bacon. Shut bag and hold it over the coals again until everything inside is cooked.

About the Author

Shirley Kurtz lives near Keyser, West Virginia, with her husband Paulson and children Jennifer, Christopher, and Zachary. She says the chickens Zachary got for his birthday, when he turned eight, were every bit as greedy as the ones in the story.

She is also the author of the children's books, *The Boy and the Quilt* and *Applesauce,* and the autobiography, *Growing Up Plain.*

About the Artist

Cheryl Benner is an artist and designer who lives near Lancaster, Pennsylvania, with her husband Lamar and sons Austin and Grant. She is co-author and designer of a series of *Country Quilt Pattern* books, as well as *Favorite Applique Patterns from The Old Country Store, Volumes 1-6.*

She is the illustrator of Kurtz's two other children's books, *The Boy and the Quilt* and *Applesauce.* She is also the illustrator of *Amos and Susie, An Amish Story.*

Cover Illustration and Design by Cheryl Benner

BIRTHDAY CHICKENS
Copyright © 1994 by Good Books
Intercourse, PA 17534

Printed in Mexico.

International Standard Book Number: 1-56148-110-6
Library of Congress Catalog Card Number: 94-24152

Library of Congress Cataloging-in-Publication Data
Kurtz, Shirley.
    Birthday chickens / by Shirley Kurtz ; illustrated by Cheryl Benner.
        p. cm.
    Summary: A boy's birthday brings him a host of chickens, whose care consumes his attention and eventually that of the entire family.
    ISBN 1-56148-110-6 (pbk.)
    [1. Chickens--Fiction.] I. Benner, Cheryl A., 1962- ill.
    II. Title.
PZ7.K9628Bi   1994
[E]--dc20   94-24152
                                                  CIP
                                                  AC